STRATTON PUBLIC LIBRARY
P.O. Box 267
Stratton, CO 80836

DATE DUE

AUG 2 1 2007		
DEC 0 5 2008		
APR 2 9 2010		
JUN 1 7 2010		
JUL 0 2 2010		
SEP 0 2 2010		

D0962187

Perma Bound 9.16

11.22

Eil
9991

The Case Of The
Big Scare
Mountain Mystery™

Look for more great books in

series:

The Case Of The Great Elephant Escape™
The Case Of The Summer Camp Caper™
The Case Of The Surfing Secret™
The Case Of The Green Ghost™

and coming soon
The Case Of The Slam Dunk Mystery™

ATTENTION: ORGANIZATIONS AND CORPORATIONS
Most HarperEntertainment books are available at special quantity discounts for bulk purchases for sales promotions, premiums, or fund-raising. For information, please call or write:
Special Markets Department, HarperCollins Publishers,
10 East 53rd Street, New York, NY 10022–5299
Telephone (212) 207-7528 Fax (212) 207-7222

The Case Of The
Big Scare
Mountain Mystery™

by Carol Ellis

■ HarperEntertainment
A Division of HarperCollins*Publishers*

A PARACHUTE PRESS BOOK

PARACHUTE PRESS

Parachute Publishing, L.L.C.
156 Fifth Avenue
New York, NY 10010

DUALSTAR PUBLICATIO

Dualstar Publications
c/o Thorne and Comp
1801 Century Park East
Los Angeles, CA 90067

HarperEntertainment
A Division of HarperCollins*Publishers*
10 East 53rd Street, New York, NY 10022–5299

Copyright © 1999 Dualstar Entertainment Group, Inc. All rights reserved.
All photography copyright © 1999 Dualstar Entertainment Group, Inc.
All rights reserved.

THE NEW ADVENTURES OF MARY-KATE & ASHLEY, THE ADVENTURES OF MARY-KATE & ASHLEY, Mary-Kate + Ashley's Fun Club, Clue and all logos, charact names and other distinctive likenesses thereof are the trademarks of Dualstar Entertainment Group, Inc. All rights reserved. THE NEW ADVENTURES OF MARY KATE & ASHLEY books created and produced by Parachute Publishing, L.L.C., in co eration with Dualstar Publications, a division of Dualstar Entertainment Group, Inc published by HarperEntertainment, a division of HarperCollins*Publishers*.

If you purchased this book without a cover, you should be aware that this book i stolen property. It was reported as "unsold and destroyed" to the publisher, and neither the author nor the publisher has received payment for this "stripped book

No part of this publication may be reproduced in whole or in part, or stored in a retrieval system, or transmitted in any form or by any means, electronic, mechanica photocopying, recording, or otherwise, without written permission of the publishe

For information, address HarperCollins Publishers Inc.
10 East 53rd Street, New York, NY 10022–5299

ISBN: 0-06-106587-0

HarperCollins®, 📖®, and HarperEntertainment™ are trademarks of
HarperCollins Publishers Inc.

First printing: November 1999

Printed in the United States of America

Visit HarperEntertainment on the World Wide Web at
http://www.harpercollins.com

10 9 8 7

THE MOUNTAIN MONSTER

"**C**an you believe the snow, Mary-Kate?" my sister Ashley said to me. She pointed out the window of our room at the Big Ski Mountain Lodge. "It's perfect for skiing!"

"I know," I agreed. "This is going to be so great. Five whole days of skiing. And I can't wait for the snowman-building contest!"

Ashley and I were at Big Ski Mountain with our whole family—except for our dog, Clue. We were really excited. It was the winter holiday. No school. No homework. No mysteries to solve.

Of course, we don't *mind* solving mysteries. We run the Olsen and Olsen Mystery Agency out of the attic of our house. We love being detectives. But we also love vacations, too.

And right now it was time to hit the slopes!

Ashley and I grabbed our parkas and hurried out of our room.

"Hey, you guys, wait up!" a voice called out.

We turned around. Natasha Benson had just come out of her room. We met her when we got here last night. She's our age, with long dark hair that she wears in a ponytail. She's been to Big Ski Mountain lots of times.

Natasha pointed at Ashley. "You're Mary-Kate, right?"

"Wrong." I laughed. "*I'm* Mary-Kate."

Natasha looked confused. No wonder. Ashley and I are twins. We look exactly alike, with strawberry-blond hair and blue eyes.

We don't act alike, though. Ashley is very logical. She likes to think and plan before she does something. I just jump right in and do it.

"Don't worry," I told Natasha. "You'll know which one of us is which after a while."

"Let's go get some breakfast," Natasha suggested. "Then I'll show you guys the best slopes. I know them all!"

The three of us started down the wide pine staircase. A man wearing a red parka passed us on his way up. He had a thick brown beard and sunglasses.

Natasha stared after him. "He is *so* cool!" She sighed.

"Who was that?" I asked.

"Didn't you recognize him? It was Tony

King, the rock star!" Natasha declared excitedly.

"Are you sure? Tony King doesn't have a beard," Ashley said.

"It's fake," Natasha said. She lowered her voice to a whisper. "He's in disguise, so his fans won't bother him."

"How do you know all this stuff?" I asked. "And how can you tell it's him? That guy didn't look anything like Tony King!"

Natasha didn't answer. She just gave us a mysterious look.

Ashley and I glanced at each other. We saw Tony King at a concert last summer. We got his autograph, too, so we stood close to him.

No way was that man Tony King, even without the beard!

Boy, Natasha had a wild imagination. Last night, she told us that another man was an escaped prisoner. She'd seen his picture on the TV show *Criminals on the Loose*.

Later, Ashley and I found out the man was the assistant manager of the lodge.

We walked through the lobby toward the dining room. "Look out!" Ashley cried.

The three of us jumped aside as a woman came rushing through the dining room doors. She wore a long white fur coat and dark glasses. She didn't even see us. She was too busy muttering into a cell phone.

"I wonder what her hurry is," I said.

"I think she's a spy," Natasha said. "Spies always wear fur coats."

I rolled my eyes at Ashley.

"Look!" Ashley pointed into the dining room. "Something's wrong."

We stared into the big room. It was full of people. But they weren't eating breakfast. They were standing around, looking totally confused.

We soon saw why—there *was* no breakfast. Three waiters stood in the middle of the room, yelling and waving their arms.

"Something must have happened in the kitchen," I said. "Let's go see!"

Ashley, Natasha, and I hurried through the crowd and peeked into the kitchen.

Whoa!

The room was a total wreck. Fruit and vegetables had been tossed out of the big steel refrigerators. Pots and pans were scattered all over the place. Smashed eggs and flour and cocoa powder covered the floor.

"What a mess!" Ashley said.

Natasha peered over my shoulder. "*I* know who did this!" she gasped. "It was the Big Scare Mountain Monster!"

2

A SIGHTING!

I stared at Natasha. "The *what?*"

"The Big Scare Mountain Monster," she repeated. "It lives in a cave and comes out only when the sun sets."

I glanced at Ashley. She rolled her eyes. Natasha must be making things up again!

"Well, whoever did this sure made a monster of a mess," I said. Ashley and I stepped carefully into the kitchen. The lodge manager, Mr. Butterfield, stood at the far end of the room. He was talking to the cook. He didn't seem to notice us.

"You know what the monster does?" Natasha asked. "When it starts to get dark, it goes out looking for anyone skiing late. Then it grabs them and drags them back to its cave."

I didn't pay much attention. I was too busy staring at the kitchen.

Who in the world did this?

A big box sat upside down in the middle of the floor. The label said it held packets of powdered hot chocolate—five hundred packets! But now the packets were all shredded, and the brown powder was all over the kitchen tiles.

"Look, Ashley." I pointed. A trail of chocolate powder led to the back door. "Whoever did this may have left footprints outside!"

We picked our way around the smashed eggs and pots and pans. Then I saw something red out of the corner of my eye. I stopped and looked more closely at it.

A hair scrunchie lay at the base of one of the cabinets. It was red with white polka dots. It had a couple of long dark hairs twisted in it. I remembered that Natasha was wearing one just like it last night.

I bent down and picked it up. "Isn't this yours?" I asked Natasha.

Natasha's face turned almost as red as the scrunchie. She shook her head. "No way," she said. "Why would one of my scrunchies be in the kitchen?"

Good question, I thought. I stuck the scrunchie in my pocket. It might be evidence.

Ashley pushed open the back door. "If there were any footprints, they're gone now," she said. "So is the cocoa trail. It snowed during the night."

I looked outside. Snow covered everything. "There goes that clue," I sighed.

"Why are you bothering to look for

clues?" Natasha demanded. "I'm telling you, I know who did this. It was the Big Scare Mountain Monster!"

Mr. Butterfield glanced up and frowned at Natasha. "Not that silly myth again!" he said. "It's been around for years. There is *no* monster. And it's Big *Ski* Mountain, not Big *Scare* Mountain."

"I saw the monster myself!" Natasha declared. "It's huge and it has long shaggy hair and it makes horrible grunting sounds. It almost grabbed *me* once."

"Come on, Natasha," Ashley said. "There's no such thing as monsters."

Natasha frowned at all of us. "There is too!" she insisted. "Just wait—you'll see!"

Mr. Butterfield shook his head. "Girls, I need you out of the kitchen," he told us. "The police are on their way. I don't want you underfoot."

Ashley nudged my arm. "I guess we don't need to investigate, since the police are on the case," she said.

"Right," I agreed. "Let's ski. Come on, Natasha!"

We grabbed our coats and headed for the slopes.

Ashley and I skied behind Natasha as she led us down one of the slopes, then across a ridge. When we reached another slope, Natasha pushed her goggles up and squinted in the glare.

"This is the best slope. See? There's nobody else around," she said, pointing down. "All you have to watch out for is the trees."

"Perfect!" I said. "Let's go!"

I dug my poles into the snow. But before I could push off, Natasha let out a shrill scream.

Ashley and I stared at her. "What's wrong?" Ashley cried.

"Look!" Natasha pointed down the slope. "It's the Big Scare Mountain Monster!"

Oh, sure, I thought. I wasn't even going to bother looking where Natasha was pointing.

Then Ashley gasped. So I looked.

I gasped, too. My heart was hammering.

A figure was disappearing into the trees. A figure *covered* with long shaggy hair that flapped in the wind!

The hairy figure scrambled along, hunched over. It looked like some kind of...monster!

Ashley and I stared at each other with our mouths open.

Could Natasha be right?

Was there really a monster on Big Ski Mountain?

3

SNOWMAN SURPRISE

"I don't believe this!" Ashley cried. "Let's try to catch up to it. I want to see what it is!"

She pushed off, heading down the slope. Natasha and I skied after her.

"What did I tell you?" Natasha shouted. "There *is* a monster. You saw it yourselves!"

I gulped. We did see *something*, that's for sure! I didn't really believe Natasha's story. But still...

Ashley stopped at the place where we

saw the figure. She bent over and stared at something in the snow.

"Look at these weird prints, Mary-Kate," she called.

I bent down to study the footprints. They were wide at the front, then they got longer and thinner until they came to a point at the back. And they were huge!

"I've never seen any prints like these before," I said.

"Me, either." Ashley pulled a tree branch aside and peered into the woods.

"Do you see anything?" I asked.

She shook her head. "Whoever it was is gone."

"Yeah, back to its cave," Natasha said.

"Maybe we should go into the woods and see if we can pick up the trail," Ashley suggested.

"No way!" Natasha cried. "I'm not going after that monster. Besides, it's almost time for the snowman-building contest."

She turned and skied down the slope toward the chair lift.

Ashley stared after her, frowning. "Do you think she was really scared?" she asked me. "Or was she just trying to keep us from looking for the monster—because she knows it wasn't really a monster we saw?"

"I don't know," I admitted. "But I sure would like to find out." I pulled off my red ski cap and hung it from the branch of a pine tree.

"There," I said. "If we come back later to look around, we'll be able to find the right spot. Come on, Ashley, let's go build some snowmen!"

A couple of hours later, Ashley and I stood back and stared at our snowmen. Actually, they were snowgirls. Twin snowgirls, with their arms linked.

"They look great," Ashley declared.

I looked at our snowtwins again. "Their necks look lumpy."

"Mufflers would cover them up," Ashley suggested.

"Good idea. I'll get them." I ran into the lodge and up to our room. Grabbing two mufflers, I started toward the stairs.

A woman was leaning against the wall a few feet away. She wore a long white fur coat, and she was talking into a cell phone.

It was the same woman who almost crashed into us outside the dining room that morning. She was facing the stairs, so she didn't see me.

"The plan is working so far!" the woman murmured into the phone. "I'm telling you, nobody has a clue what's coming."

A clue about what? I wondered.

The woman paused, then said, "Right. I can't talk any more now. I have to make sure the monster—"

The *monster?* I gasped.

The woman whirled around. When she saw me, she clapped the phone shut and stared at me suspiciously.

Whoa, I thought as I hurried past her. She actually said the word "monster." What did she mean?

I wished she had finished her sentence. If only I hadn't gasped!

I told Ashley about the woman as we wrapped our mufflers around the snow-twins. "Weird," she said. "I wonder what she was talking about."

"Me, too," I said. "And she said, 'Nobody has a clue what's coming.' I sure would like to know what she meant by *that!*"

We went into the lodge. The dining room and kitchen were back to normal, so we ate lunch. We went snowboarding and skiing all afternoon. By the time dinner was over, we were wiped out!

"Let's go to bed," Ashley suggested. "I want to get up early to go skiing."

"Me, too," I said. "They announce the snowman-building contest winners at ten. We can ski for an hour before that."

We said good night to our family and headed up to our room. Ashley went into the bathroom to take a shower. I changed into my fluffy yellow robe and curled up in a chair by the window.

Our window looked down on the snowmen. I was searching for ours, when I saw Natasha walking down there.

I tapped on the glass, but she didn't hear me. Then Ashley came out of the shower. "Your turn," she said, rubbing her hair with a towel.

As I stood under the hot water, I forgot all about Natasha.

Until the next morning.

Ashley and I got up early. As we started down to the dining room for a quick breakfast, we heard people shouting outside. We ran out…and found a total disaster.

All the snowmen had been smashed!

The only thing left were lumps of snow. The twigs used for arms, rocks for eyes and mouths, carrot noses, and many pieces of colorful clothing were scattered all over.

Three young birch trees near the snowmen were bent completely to the ground. One of them had even snapped in two.

"It looks like a hurricane hit!" Ashley exclaimed.

Mr. Butterfield gazed at the mess. He ran his hands through his hair until it stood straight up. "This is terrible!" he groaned. "The snowman-building contest is one of our biggest attractions!"

We began to walk around the wrecked snowmen. Suddenly, Ashley grabbed my arm. "Mary-Kate, look at those footprints!"

I bent down and checked out the four big footprints. "They're like the ones we saw yesterday," I said. "Except they don't get long and narrow at the back."

Ashley glanced around. "Let's see if we can find some more."

We walked carefully, peering at the ground. We found a few more of the big prints. But most of them had been trampled by other people.

Natasha ran up to us. "The monster!" she cried. "The monster was here. He came during the night and wrecked everything!"

Mr. Butterfield frowned at her. "Please, keep your voice down, young lady. People are getting nervous. Five families have left already!"

"You mean people believe the story about the monster?" Ashley asked him.

"They don't know *what* to believe!" Mr. Butterfield moaned.

"What do the police say?" I asked.

"That it's probably a prankster," Mr. Butterfield replied. "But they're very busy. They have only one officer to work on this case. And *he* can't get here until later today.

This is terrible for business. I need to find whoever is doing this—fast!"

"Maybe my sister and I can help," Ashley said. "We're detectives."

"You are?" Natasha gasped. "Wow!"

"We've solved lots of cases," I added. "We'll be glad to try to solve this one."

"That's very sweet of you, girls…" Mr. Butterfield began.

I could see that he wasn't sure what to say. That happens sometimes with grown-ups. After all, we are only ten years old.

"We promise we won't get in the police's way," I said. "We'll just look around and see what we can find out."

"Well…" Mr. Butterfield shrugged. "I need all the help I can get." He shook hands with Ashley and me. "You're hired!"

Ashley and I grinned at each other.

The Trenchcoat Twins were on the case!

4

TRAPPED!

"**O**kay, let's list our suspects," Ashley said. We were up in our room at the lodge. "I didn't bring my detective notebook on vacation. Did you bring your tape recorder?"

"Nope," I said. I usually use a mini tape recorder to take my case notes. But I left it at home.

Ashley opened the desk drawer. She pulled out a pen and a folder full of lodge stationery. She wrote the word SUSPECTS at the top of a piece of paper.

"Natasha is definitely a suspect," I said. "I found a scrunchie just like hers in the kitchen, with two dark hairs in it." I snapped my fingers. "*And* there's something else. I saw her walking around the snowmen last night. That means she was in both places before they were wrecked."

Next to Natasha's name, Ashley wrote, CLUES: SCRUNCHIE IN THE KITCHEN, SEEN NEAR SNOWMEN. Then she wrote the word MOTIVE. "Why would Natasha do this stuff?" she asked.

"That's easy. Because she wants people to think there really is a monster," I replied. "Remember how mad she got when nobody believed her? She said, 'Just wait—you'll see.'"

Ashley nodded. "I remember. But would she really do all this stuff just to make us believe her story?"

"I'm not sure," I admitted. "But I guess

we have to check her out."

"We have to investigate the lady in the white fur coat, too," Ashley said. "The way she keeps whispering into her cell phone, she's definitely hiding something."

"Right. And don't forget that mystery person or monster or whatever it was we saw on the slope yesterday," I said. "Those giant footprints were in both places."

Ashley frowned. "But the prints we found by the snowmen didn't match the ones on the slope. They were the same size—huge! But they didn't get narrow at the back."

"Are you saying there's a fourth suspect?" I asked. "Someone we don't even know about?"

Ashley doodled on the top of her note page. "It doesn't make sense."

"Great-Grandma Olive would say that's why it's a mystery," I pointed out.

Our great-grandmother is a detective,

too. She taught us everything we know about solving mysteries.

Grinning, Ashley wrote down a big question mark. "Okay, we'll start with the suspects we know."

But when we went looking for Natasha, we discovered that she and her parents went into town for the afternoon. And we didn't know where the fur coat lady was.

That left the strange figure on the ski slope.

We decided to see if we could track him—or it—down. We headed back upstairs to get our coats.

As we started down the hall, we saw the fur coat lady leave her room. She had her cell phone out, as usual. She punched numbers into it and swept past us, frowning.

Ashley nudged me in the arm. "Look! She left her door open!"

"This is our chance!" I whispered to her. "I'll stand guard. You check the place out!"

Ashley glanced up and down the hall. Then she dashed into the room. I stood in the doorway to keep watch.

"Hey!" Ashley cried after a couple of seconds. "Look at this!"

I quickly glanced into the room. Ashley held up a bunch of paper packets. I squinted to read the labels.

Instant cocoa! Just like the stuff all over the kitchen floor.

"These were on the nightstand," Ashley said. "And there are two full boxes of them on the dresser. What is she doing with all this cocoa?"

I didn't answer—because I heard something. Footsteps!

I glanced down the hall. Oh, no!

The fur coat lady appeared at the top of the stairs!

She had her head down, so she didn't see me. But she would definitely see us if we ran out of her room.

There was only one thing to do.

I ducked into the room. "Quick! Hide!" I whispered. "She's coming!"

Ashley dropped the cocoa onto the nightstand. I glanced frantically around for a hiding place. The closet was no good—what if she opened it?

"The bed!" Ashley grabbed my arm and pulled me to the floor. We slithered under the bed. I held my breath.

The footsteps came closer. I saw the woman's black high-heeled boots in the doorway. She strode into the room.

And headed straight for the bed!

"I know you're there!" she declared angrily.

5

THE CONFUSING CALL

Oh, no!

We were caught!

How were we ever going to explain this?

I saw one of her black boot tap the floor impatiently. "Come on," the woman said.

Then she sat on the bed!

What was she doing? Was she going to sit there until we crawled out?

"I really need to talk to you," she said. "It's important. Pick up the phone!"

What? The *phone?*

The woman was talking on her cell phone. She didn't catch us after all!

"Please pick up—this is *very* important," the woman said.

I heard the sound of the nightstand drawer opening and closing. Then I heard some beeping sounds. I figured she must be punching numbers into the phone.

"This is Dana Hartwick," the woman said. "I've been trying to reach Fred, but he won't pick up the phone. So I need to speak to you. Call me back as soon as possible."

The springs creaked as Dana Hartwick stood up. I watched her black boots tap toward the door. As she disappeared from sight, a piece of paper fluttered to the floor. It must have fallen from her pocket.

The door clicked shut. "That was close!" Ashley whispered.

"*Too* close," I agreed. "Let's get out of here before she comes back again!"

We scooted out and jumped to our feet. I

snatched up the piece of paper as we dashed across the room.

Ashley stuck her head out the door and looked up and down the hall. "All clear!"

We hurried out.

"What's on the piece of paper Dana Hartwick dropped?" Ashley asked when we got into our room.

I smoothed it out and looked at it. "It's a phone number. No name," I told her.

Ashley shrugged. "Let's call it."

I picked up our phone and punched in the number from the paper. It rang four times...five...I was almost ready to hang up, when someone finally picked up.

"Animal Magnetism, Hollywood office," a woman said. I could hear lots of weird noises in the background. "May I help you?"

Hollywood? "Um...I'm not sure," I said.

"What kind of talent are you looking for?" she asked. She sounded impatient. "I'm sure our agency will have it."

"Uh, well—I—I—" I stammered.

"Oh! Look out—he's escaping!" the woman on the other end cried suddenly. Then—*click!* The line went dead.

"Whoa!" Ashley said when I told her about it. "Who's escaping? Call back!"

I punched in the number again. But the line was busy.

I waited a minute and tried again.

"It's still busy." I hung up. "I'm totally confused. What do Dana Hartwick and a weird talent agency have to do with what's going on here at Big Ski Mountain?"

"Maybe nothing," Ashley said. "But whether they're connected or not, Dana Hartwick is definitely involved in something very weird. We have to find out more about her."

"Right," I agreed. I grinned. "And I just thought of the perfect place to start!"

THE COCOA TRAIL

"I saw Ms. Hartwick go through here about half an hour ago," the check-in clerk told us. "Look in the dining room."

"We already did," I said quickly.

We weren't really looking for Dana Hartwick. We wanted to find out whatever we could about her. But we were trying to be casual about it.

"One place you *won't* find her is out on the slopes." The clerk shook his head. "She hasn't been skiing since yesterday morning.

when she got here. All she does is whisper into that phone of hers. I don't know what she's doing at a ski resort."

I raised my eyebrows. Dana Hartwick seemed weirder and weirder!

"Wait a minute," Ashley said. "Did you say she got here yesterday morning?"

"That's right," the clerk replied. "I remember, because the lodge sent a car to pick her up at the airport. She flew in from California, you know. Hollywood!"

Hollywood? I thought. *Maybe she works for Animal Magnetism.*

"She went straight to the dining room for breakfast." The clerk shrugged. "Of course, that was the morning we found the kitchen torn apart, so she was out of luck."

We thanked the clerk and moved away from the desk. "That means she couldn't have wrecked the kitchen," Ashley said to me. "She didn't get here in time."

"I know. I guess we can cross her off our

list of suspects." I sighed. "It's too bad—she seems *so* suspicious!"

"Let's see if we can find that weird hairy person," Ashley said.

We put our boots and skis on. Outside, it was windy, with dark clouds piled up in the sky. As we pushed off down the slope, it started to snow.

After a little while I spotted my red ski cap hanging on the spruce tree branch where I'd left it.

We skied to the hat and stopped. In front of us was the beginning of a narrow trail.

The snow on the trail was packed down hard. I couldn't see any footprints. We slipped and slid along on our skis.

Not much light came through the branches. The wind whistled in the tree-tops. It was a lonely sound.

I shivered. "Maybe this isn't such a good idea, Ashley," I said nervously. "What if we get lost or something?"

"How can we?" Ashley asked. "All we do is follow the trail back to your cap."

I knew Ashley was right. But I still felt nervous. What if there were a blizzard and we couldn't get out? What if we ran into a mountain lion, or a bear, or…a monster?

All of a sudden, I wasn't so sure Natasha's monster story was made up!

"Look, Mary-Kate." Ashley pointed. "See that little line of brown stuff on the trail? It looks like whoever went through here spilled dirt or something."

We pushed ahead to the thin line of dirt. Ashley bent down and peered at it. Then she sniffed it.

"Hey!" she exclaimed. "I think this is cocoa!"

Whoa. Cocoa in the kitchen. Cocoa in Dana's room. Now cocoa in the woods.

"This case is full of cocoa!" I said.

The line of brown powder snaked down the trail as far as I could see. I was still very nervous, but no way would I turn back now!

Ashley and I skied through the woods. The trail twisted and turned. The line of cocoa powder twisted and turned with it.

The trail led us to a small clearing. On one side was a low hill with some dead trees piled in front of it. There was a small pile of cocoa powder in front of the trees.

I stooped down and peered through the branches. "I see an opening, Ashley. Maybe there's a tunnel in here or something."

We began pulling some of the trees away. After a minute, we could see the opening. It wasn't a tunnel.

It was a cave.

"This is creepy," I whispered. "Natasha said the monster lived in a cave."

"What should we do?" Ashley asked. Her voice shook a little.

I swallowed hard. I didn't want to go into that dark cave.

But we had a mystery to solve. We couldn't just ski away from it!

"We have to check it out," I said.

"Right," Ashley agreed.

We both took out our penlights. But as we started to step into the cave, we heard a crashing noise behind us. Branches snapped. Frozen snow crackled.

I whirled around.

A huge, hairy figure leaped out of the woods. It bounded forward, roaring.

"Aaahhh!" Ashley and I screamed.

It was coming straight at us!

We were monster meat!

7

ANOTHER SUSPECT!

"**R**un, Ashley!" I cried.

"That's right, *run away!*" the creature bellowed.

We spun around. The mouth of the cave yawned in front of us.

"We're trapped!" I moaned. I grabbed Ashley's hand. "We'll have to fight!"

But Ashley didn't move. She just stood there with a confused look on her face. "Wait," she said. "A monster that *talks*?"

Huh? We turned back around.

The creature loomed over us. It was *very* tall and covered with fur. My eyes were level with its waist.

My gaze traveled slowly up its furry chest to its face. Tangled brown hair hung over its forehead. Fierce eyes glared at us through a pair of beat-up sunglasses.

Sunglasses?

Ashley nudged me. "I have never heard of a monster wearing sunglasses," she whispered. She pointed at its feet. "Or snowshoes."

My heartbeat began to slow down. *It's not a monster*, I realized. *It's a man!*

I stared at the man. Long tangled hair hung down past his shoulders. A thick brown beard grew down to his chest.

But the rest of the "hair" on his body was a dark, ratty fur coat that came all the way down to his ankles. He wore ancient-looking snowshoes. They came to a long point at the back.

The man flapped his hands at us. "Go on!" he shouted. "Get away! You don't see me snooping around *your* home, do you?"

"You mean...you *live* in this cave?" Ashley asked.

"That's right," he snapped. "What's wrong with that?"

"Nothing," I said quickly. "Caves are fine!"

"They're better than fine!" he said with a scowl. "No cars. No noise. No people. Caves are perfect!"

"Uh—right," Ashley said. She nudged me with her ski pole.

"You don't believe me?" he asked. "Take a look!" He swung his knapsack off his shoulder. He took out a big flashlight and shined it into the mouth of the cave. "Go on—look!"

Ashley and I stepped out of our ski bindings. I peered into the cave.

It was actually kind of cozy. There was a cot with a thick sleeping bag on it, and a wood-burning stove with a chimney hole cut in the roof. Some wooden shelves held cans and boxes of food.

"It's very nice, Mr.…um…" Ashley said.

"Call me Charlie," he said. He stomped past us and went inside. He put a log into the stove and sat down on the cot.

Ashley and I stayed in the mouth of the cave. I wanted to be able to run if we needed to!

"We didn't mean to bother you," I said. "See, we're staying at Big Ski Mountain Lodge and—"

"Don't talk to me about that lodge!" he grumbled. "It's the worst thing that ever happened. Too many people—they're all over the mountain!"

Ashley nudged me and pointed to the shelves of food.

Whoa! I thought. There was a big box of

instant cocoa.

Charlie saw us staring at it. "Want some, eh?" he said. To my surprise, a smile spread across his bearded face. "That's right—children always like cocoa. Well, let's see if there's enough here for three cups."

Charlie took down the box and pulled off the lid. He peered inside. "Dratted thing came open in my knapsack on the way back from the store. Dribbled cocoa all the way here," he muttered. "But I think there's enough left for the three of us."

Charlie lifted a battered kettle off the woodstove. As he poured hot water into three tin mugs, Ashley leaned close to me. "That could explain the cocoa trail," she whispered. "But he also could have stolen the cocoa from the lodge."

Charlie handed us each a mug of hot chocolate. "So you went to the store yesterday?" Ashley asked. "The one in town?"

Charlie nodded. "Long trip. Had to sleep

at the store."

Ashley and I glanced at each other. I knew what she was thinking. If Charlie was telling the truth, then he didn't smash the snowmen. He wasn't anywhere near the lodge last night.

We would have to check out his story. But I hoped he was telling the truth. He looked weird—but I kind of liked him.

"What about the night before?" I asked. That was when the kitchen got wrecked. "Were you in town then, too?"

Charlie shook his head. "I was fishing up at Rainbow Lake. Came back yesterday."

"Fishing? Isn't the lake frozen?" Ashley asked.

"*Ice* fishing," Charlie told her. He gave us a sharp look. "Why are you two asking so many questions?"

"No reason," I said. "We're just curious."

"You mean *nosy*," he muttered. "That's the trouble with people. They won't leave a person alone. And it's getting worse and worse since that lodge was built!"

He seemed to be getting mad again. I set down my mug. "Let's go, Ashley," I murmured. We stepped back into our skis.

"Better be careful," Charlie said. "It's dangerous to be out in these woods. Didn't you hear about that boy?"

"What...what boy?" I stammered.

Charlie gave a creepy cackle. "It happened right in front of the ski lodge. A boy your age disappeared—and he was never seen again! They say the mountain monster got him."

I gulped.

Charlie leaned close and glared at us. "Watch out—or you just might disappear yourselves!"

8

STRANDED ON THE SKI LIFT

"That was creepy!" Ashley gasped as we hurried through the woods.

"It was," I agreed. "And just when I was starting to like him!"

We pushed along the trail as fast as we could. I kept glancing over my shoulder in case Charlie was following us.

We finally reached the end of the woods. As we burst out of the trees, the wind almost knocked us over. The snow was coming down harder.

We skied down to the lift and climbed on. It gave a jerk and started up toward the lodge. We were the only ones on it. Everyone else must have stopped skiing when the snowstorm got bad.

"I think that Charlie is our number one suspect," Ashley said.

I nodded. "It is very suspicious that there's a cocoa trail leading back to his cave. Plus, he has a motive for wrecking the kitchen—he *really* hates the ski lodge."

Ashley nodded. "Maybe he's trying to scare people away. If enough customers stop coming, the lodge will eventually go out of business. Charlie would be happy then."

"I feel kind of bad for him," I said. "All he wants is to be left alone. I wish we could help him somehow." I sighed. "But we *do* have to check out his story."

"I don't know how we can check out whether he was at Rainbow Lake," Ashley said. "Who would we ask—the fish?"

I snuggled my hands deeper into my jacket pockets. "But we can call the general store and find out if he was really there last night," I said.

A big gust of wind came up. The chair swung wildly.

"Whoa!" I cried. I peered down through the swirling snow. The ground was *way* too far away!

Ashley pointed up ahead. "Isn't that the lodge?"

I peered through the blowing snow. I finally saw the dark outlines of the big lodge building. Somebody was hurrying away from it, but I couldn't tell who it was.

The figure dashed down a path into the woods. "Who would want to take a walk in this storm?" Ashley wondered.

The wind gusted forcefully. The chair swung like crazy. Ashley and I ducked our heads and held on tight.

I suddenly felt a strong jerk. At first I thought it was the wind blowing our chair. But then I realized—we weren't moving.

"What's going on?" I asked nervously. We weren't at the top of the slope yet. "Why did we stop?"

"Don't worry," Ashley said. "I'm sure we'll move again in a few seconds."

A few seconds passed. We didn't move.

My teeth chattered. My nose felt like a blob of ice.

A few more seconds went by. A minute. Two minutes. Three...four.

The lift still didn't move.

"Ummm, Ashley?" I said, trying to keep my voice steady. "Are you thinking what I'm thinking?"

"I don't know." Ashley sounded worried. "What are you thinking?"

I gulped. "I'm thinking—we're stuck up here!"

CONFRONTING THE SUSPECTS

The lift swung and twisted in the wind.

"What are we going to do?" I cried. "We can't jump! We're at least fifty feet in the air!"

"Just hang on, Mary-Kate!" Ashley shouted. "Somebody will figure out that the lift is stuck!"

But when? I wondered.

The chair rocked and swayed in the wind. My fingers grew numb. Soon I couldn't even feel my nose anymore!

I peered down through the snow. That was the wrong thing to do! It made me even more scared. I quickly closed my eyes.

"What's taking so long?" I cried. "Why doesn't somebody tell the lift worker that it's stuck?"

"Maybe no one knows," Ashley said. "We're the only ones *on* the lift."

Oh, no! I thought.

"Plus, the snow is so thick, I bet no one can see us!" Ashley added.

"Stop being so logical!" I told her. "We have to *do* something!"

"Like what?"

"Like scream for help!" I leaned over the side of the chair. *"Help!"* I shouted. *"We're trapped on the lift! Somebody help!"*

The lift suddenly gave a big jerk. Then it slowly began climbing up again.

Ashley and I sighed with relief when we finally reached the top. As we hopped off, we saw one of the lodge workers walking toward us.

"Thank goodness you fixed the lift!" I cried. "We were stranded up in the air for fifteen minutes!"

"I'm sorry about that," he said. "But it's not broken. It was turned off."

"Huh? Why?" I asked.

"I don't know. It's not supposed to be," he replied. "One of the ground crew noticed it and turned it back on. Weird, huh?"

"Very weird!" Ashley said.

We quickly got our skis off. We hurried into the lodge and stamped our feet to warm them up.

"Remember what we saw when we were stuck up there?" Ashley asked. "Someone running into the woods? Whoever it was, they ran right by the ski lift controls. That's where that path leads—right to the control booth."

"And right after that, the lift stopped," I said. "Wow. Do you think somebody did it on purpose?"

"If they did, there's only one reason," Ashley declared. "To scare us so we'll stop investigating."

"So maybe it was Charlie," I said.

Ashley shook her head. "I don't see how he could have gotten up to the lodge so fast. But I guess he might know a shortcut."

"Or it could have been Natasha. We haven't crossed her off our suspect list yet," I pointed out.

"Well, now's our chance." Ashley pointed toward the dining room. Natasha was at a table by herself, eating a grilled cheese sandwich.

"Come on, Mary-Kate," Ashley said. "It's time to get some answers!"

10

CHECKING THE FACTS

"Hi, Natasha." I pulled out a chair and sat down across from her. Ashley sat on her right.

The waiter came over. We ordered cheeseburgers and hot apple cider. "Did you have a good time in town?" I asked Natasha.

"I didn't go," she said. "I went snow-boarding until it started snowing so hard."

"Did you see the monster?" Ashley asked. She leaned forward.

"No." Natasha scowled. "You guys don't even believe in the monster, so don't kid around with me," she said.

"Well, something wrecked the kitchen and the snowmen," I said. "Or some*one*." I stared at her.

"Don't look at me," Natasha said angrily. "*I* didn't do it!"

"Then what was your scrunchie doing in the kitchen?" Ashley asked.

Natasha blushed and fiddled with her sandwich. "I told you—it wasn't my scrunchie," she mumbled.

"Yes, it was," I said. "I saw you wearing it the other day. And it had long dark hairs twisted around it. You were definitely in the kitchen that night."

"That makes you a suspect," Ashley said.

"Okay—I admit it!" Natasha cried. "I went to the kitchen. But all I did was take some cookies. I didn't wreck anything. The place was totally fine when I left!"

"What about the snowmen?" I asked. "I saw you out there with them the night they got smashed."

"I wanted to fix my snowgirl. Her skirt was lopsided," Natasha said. "I fixed it and left—and that's all! I didn't touch any other snowmen. And I didn't wreck the kitchen. I would never do anything like that! I can't believe you guys think I would!"

Natasha jumped up from her chair and stomped out of the dining room.

The waiter brought our cheeseburgers and cider.

I drank some cider. "I kind of believe her," I said.

"Me, too," Ashley agreed. "She could have done those things, but she doesn't really have a motive. I don't think she would cause so much trouble just to prove there's a monster."

"So Natasha is out, and Dana Hartwick is out," I said. I leaned back in my chair.

"That leaves us with with one suspect—Charlie."

After lunch the next day, Ashley and I climbed into a white van that had BIG SKI MOUNTAIN painted on the sides. The lodge kept a bunch of vans to drive people into town.

It was still snowing. The van was full because lots of people were going into town instead of skiing. They probably wanted to buy stuff like socks and mittens and toothpaste.

Ashley and I wanted to solve a mystery.

The van dropped us off at Bob's General Store. It was in a big house with wooden floors and barrels of candy.

We filled a bag with lemon drops and took it to the counter. The man at the cash register smiled at us.

"Excuse me," I said. "Are you Bob?"

"Yup," he said. "How did you know?"

"Charlie told us," I replied.

"Charlie?" he asked in surprise. "He *talked* to you?"

Ashley nodded. "Mostly, he talked about how much he hates the lodge."

"He wishes it had never been built." Bob chuckled. "But it's a little late for that."

"We need to know where Charlie was the night before last," Ashley said.

"We're detectives," I explained. "Mr. Butterfield, the lodge manager, asked us to work on a case for him."

"Is that right?" Bob asked, chuckling.

"Did you hear about the lodge snowmen getting wrecked?" Ashley asked.

"Sure. Don't tell me you young ladies think Charlie did it!" Bob said.

"That's what we're trying to find out," I said. "He told us he slept here that night."

"He sure did," Bob said. "He stays at the store whenever he comes in for supplies. Of course, he doesn't really sleep *in* the store. He won't stay inside a real house. He rolls up in his sleeping bag on the back porch. But I heard him snoring there all night. Kept me awake!"

"Are you sure?" Ashley asked.

"Positive," Bob declared. "Trust me—Charlie isn't your man."

Ashley and I thanked him and walked outside. Ashley gave me a frustrated look.

"You know what this means, don't you?" she asked.

I nodded.

Charlie was the only suspect we had left. And now *he* was off the list.

We were fresh out of suspects!

A *SECOND* MONSTER?!

"**W**e must be missing something," I said when the van arrived back at the lodge late that afternoon.

"We're missing suspects." Ashley sighed.

"I know, but we can't give up," I told her. "Let's go over all your notes again."

We got out of the van. As we walked toward the lodge, a sudden flash of white caught my eye. It was Dana Hartwick in her white fur coat.

We stopped and watched. Dana walked

out of the woods and hurried into the lodge through a side door. She was talking into her cell phone, as usual.

I suddenly had an idea. "She's talking on the phone!"

"Huh? So what?" Ashley asked. "She's always on the phone."

"Right. And maybe she's talking to the person who actually wrecked the kitchen," I said. "Dana Hartwick didn't have to be here that night. She could have planned it with somebody else!"

"I never thought of that," Ashley said.

"Maybe we crossed Dana Hartwick off the list too soon," I declared. "We might have a suspect after all!"

We walked toward the lodge. As we passed the ski lift, we noticed that it wasn't moving.

Then one of the workers brushed a big blob of heavy, wet snow off the starter switch. The lift began moving again.

"Maybe that's why we got stuck," I said.

"Or maybe Dana Hartwick turned the switch off." Ashley pointed toward the woods. "That's where she just came out, right? It's the same place we saw someone go *into* the woods before we got stuck."

We turned away from the lodge and ran toward the woods. Hidden among the trees was a narrow path.

"Let's see where this leads!" Ashley said.

We ducked into the woods and started along the path. The snow was coming down hard. The wind whistled, and the trees creaked all around us.

Snow fell from a tree limb onto my head. I brushed it off and shivered. "We're getting pretty far from the lodge," I said.

"Yeah, and it's getting pretty dark, too," Ashley said. "Maybe this wasn't such a good idea."

More snow plopped onto my head. Bits of ice went down my collar. "Let's do this tomorrow morning," I said with another shiver. "We can just keep an eye on Dana until then."

We started to turn around.

"Uunnggh! Uunnnngh!" A loud, weird grunting sound echoed through the woods.

Ashley and I froze in our tracks.

"UUNNNGH!" The grunting noise came again. It was louder this time. And closer.

"It's coming from right over there!" I shouted. I pointed ahead.

Then something moved.

A huge, hairy white creature with a giant, weirdly shaped head lumbered down the path.

I screamed as it reached out its giant claws—and tried to grab us!

12

POLAR POSSIBILITIES

"**A**aahhh!" Ashley and I both screamed.

"Unnngghh!" the creature grunted. Its huge, weirdly-shaped head bobbed up and down. "Unnngghhh!"

"Go!" I spun around and grabbed Ashley's arm. *"Go!"*

We raced back down the path and burst out of the woods. We didn't stop running until we were inside the lodge.

"What *was* that?" Ashley gasped. "It looked like a…"

"Like a *monster!*" I said.

"Exactly!" Ashley was shaking.

I couldn't believe it. Was Natasha actually right? Was there really a Big Scare Mountain Monster? Did the monster wreck the kitchen and the snowmen?

I didn't know what to think. All I *did* know was that I planned to spend the rest of the evening in our nice, safe, cozy room!

The next morning, Ashley shook me awake. She was already dressed. "Get up!" she said. "We still have a mystery to solve!"

I sat up in bed. "What about the thing we saw last night?"

"Well, I was thinking," Ashley said as I pulled on a pair of jeans and a sweater. "Even if there really is a monster, Dana Hartwick is still a suspect. Remember how she was talking on the phone to someone about 'the monster'? And remember how we saw her coming from the spot in the woods where we ran into that thing last night? Whatever is going on, I think Dana Hartwick has something to do with it."

When we went into the dining room for breakfast, Ashley nudged me. "Look! There she is."

Dana Hartwick sat at a table, studying a bunch of papers. Her cell phone was on the table, but for once she wasn't talking on it.

We walked to a nearby table. As we passed Dana, she slipped the papers into a folder and snapped it shut.

Ashley and I sat down. "We have to see what's in that folder," she whispered to me. "It could give us some clue about what she's up to."

"Right," I said. "You distract her. I'll get the folder."

Ashley jumped up and hurried toward Dana's table. As she passed the table, she "accidentally" bumped into it.

Dana's phone flew off the table and landed

with a clatter on the floor.

"My phone!" Dana jumped up.

"I'm sorry!" Ashley said. She ran to pick up the phone and "accidentally" kicked it all the way to the other side of the room.

"Be careful!" Dana cried.

"I'm really sorry!" Ashley said. "I'll get it for you."

Dana scooted out from behind her table and followed Ashley across the room.

Now was my chance!

I slipped over to Dana's table and quickly opened the folder.

Inside were a bunch of snapshots of…a polar bear!

One of the pictures showed the bear gliding downhill on a sled. In another one, he was sitting on top of a cooler.

In every picture, he held a big yellow mug in his paw. Below the pictures were the words, "Polar Cocoa—Wally Says It's the Best!"

Cocoa—again!

I glanced across the dining room. Ashley and Dana were down on their hands and knees, peering under a table.

I checked out the pictures again. They all had labels on them that said PROPERTY OF ANIMAL MAGNETISM.

Hmmm. That was the name of that Hollywood agency!

I stared at Wally. Big and white...

Could *he* be the creature Ashley and I saw last night? But what would a polar bear be doing in the Rocky Mountains?

"There it is!" Ashley suddenly said in a loud voice.

I was out of time! I quickly shuffled the photos into the folder and scurried back to my table.

By the time Dana and Ashley returned, I was reading a menu.

"Good work," I whispered to Ashley when she sat down.

Ashley grinned. "She never suspected a thing. What was in the folder?"

I told her about the polar bear pictures with the ANIMAL MAGNETISM label.

"Hmmm," Ashley said. "Maybe Animal Magnetism is an *animal* talent agency. Wally the polar bear could be one of their animal actors."

"Right! So…" I frowned. "What does it mean?"

Ashley sighed. "I still don't have a clue!"

Just then, Dana Hartwick walked past our table. She hurried toward the front door.

Ashley and I jumped up and followed her. *Solve the case first*, I thought. *Eat later!*

We hurried out of the lodge. Dana was walking into the woods—toward the spot where we saw the monster!

We ran across the snow and ducked into the woods. Ahead of us, we could hear

Dana's footsteps crunching on the snow and ice.

Crunch, crunch, crunch. Dana marched quickly along the path. "She's not out for a stroll, that's for sure," I whispered. "She's walking too fast."

Crunch, crunch, crunch. Dana kept walking.

We stayed close behind her. It was hard to be quiet. But Dana was making so much noise, I figured she couldn't hear us.

Crunch, crunch...

After about ten minutes, the footsteps stopped.

Ashley and I froze and listened.

Everything stayed quiet.

Where did Dana go?

We slowly moved forward. I spotted a clearing up ahead. My heart started to pound.

We crept closer to the clearing. A small log cabin sat in the center. Next to it was a huge metal cage. And in the cage sat a snowy-white polar bear!

I stared at the bear. He was wearing a pair of silver moonboots on his hind feet. A white, furry, Russian-style hat sat on his head.

"Guess what?" I whispered. "We just found our monster!"

THE SNOWY SECRET UNCOVERED

Ashley and I stepped out from the trees. When the bear caught sight of us, it let out a grunt. "Unnnngghhh!"

Wham!

The door to the cabin flew open. Dana Hartwick burst out.

"Promise me!" she cried. "Please promise me you won't tell! This just has to stay secret!"

"What has to stay secret?" I asked.

"The commercial I'm directing for Polar

Cocoa," Dana said. "It's top secret. I want the whole world to be surprised when it goes on the air!"

"You mean because you're using a polar bear?" I asked.

Dana nodded. "We're filming later today. Thank goodness it's sunny. We've postponed the shoot for days because of the bad weather! The monster is getting tired of waiting."

"The monster? Do you mean the bear?" Ashley asked.

"Of course. He's very spoiled—that's why I call him that," Dana explained. "His name is Wally."

I looked at Wally. "Why is he wearing that hat and those moonboots?"

"His ears and feet get cold," Dana replied. "Like I said, he's spoiled. But he's a wonderful actor."

"Uunngghh!" Wally grunted again.

The cabin door opened, and a man came

out. He carried a big jug in one hand and a plastic bag in the other.

"This is Mike, Wally's trainer," Dana said. "He's bringing the monster his breakfast."

"Raw fish and cocoa," Mike said. He stopped and showed it to Ashley and me. "He gets it every morning."

Phew! The fish really smelled!

Wally bounced up and down in his moonboots, grunting. He put his paws up against the bars of his cage.

"He's crazy about cocoa," Mike told us. "In a minute, Wally!"

"That's why I picked him," Dana said. "He's a perfect 'spokesbear' for Polar Cocoa."

"Ungghhh!"

We all looked at Wally.

The huge bear must have gotten tired of waiting for his breakfast. He stuck his paw through the bars of his cage, unlatched the door, and lumbered into the clearing!

Dana and Mike gasped. Mike ran to the cage and set the fish and cocoa inside. Wally hurried back in and slurped down some cocoa.

Mike latched the door again. "I had no idea he could do that!"

"I think he's unlocked that cage more than once," Ashley said. "I think Wally is the Big Scare Mountain Monster!"

"Right!" I exclaimed. Everything finally made sense!

"The *what?*" Mike cried.

Ashley and I both explained.

"See, Wally knows how to let himself out of the cage. And he's just been hanging around, waiting for the shoot, for a long time," Ashley said. "He got bored."

"So he must have let himself out at night and wandered around Big Ski Mountain," I put in. "One night he broke into the kitchen at the ski lodge and helped himself to cocoa and stuff from the refrigerators."

"And the next night he smashed all the snowmen from the contest," Ashley added. "I guess that's how bears play."

"And his moonboots left giant, weird footprints—we couldn't figure out what kind of animal would make them," I said.

"And the thing we saw last night was Wally—keeping his head warm with a fur hat!" Ashley finished. "Boy, will Mr. Butterfield be relieved when we explain what's happening."

"We have to tell Mr. Butterfield," I said to Dana. "But we won't say a word to anybody else about your commercial."

Dana thanked us. Then she invited us to come see the filming. It was being done in a hidden valley a few miles from the ski lodge. She gave us careful directions.

Mike thanked us, too. "I could have lost my favorite bear!"

"I don't think so," Ashley told him. "Wally always came back, didn't he? He didn't want to miss his favorite breakfast!"

Later that afternoon, we headed for the shoot. Natasha was with us. Dana said it was all right for her to come, too, as long as she kept the commercial a secret.

I hoped Natasha would be able to keep her mouth shut for once!

As we walked through the woods, we spotted a figure moving in the distance. It was Charlie the hermit on his snowshoes.

Charlie! We ran to catch up with him. "Remember us?" Ashley asked.

Charlie nodded. "I'm in a hurry," he grumbled.

"Don't worry, we won't talk long," I said. "We just wanted to tell you some good news. We talked to Mr. Butterfield at the lodge, and he agreed to close the ski slope near your cave. He says it's too hard to keep it groomed, anyway. So there won't be as many people bothering you."

Charlie's jaw dropped. "You don't say! Why, I—I—" he stammered. "That's the nicest thing anyone ever did for me!"

"We also found out who was doing all those things at the lodge," Ashley added. "It wasn't a monster, it was a polar bear." She frowned. "There's just one thing we never did figure out. What happened to that boy who disappeared all those years ago? Did a monster really take him?"

Charlie hesitated. "Well, you did a good turn for me, so I reckon I can do one for you," he said. He cleared his throat. "The truth is, there never was any boy who disappeared. I made the whole story up."

"You did?" Natasha gasped.

Charlie's face turned red. "See, Big Ski Mountain is my home—and it's getting too crowded. I spread that monster story to scare people away. Never worked, though." He shrugged. "And to tell you the truth, there are some people I don't mind—like you kids. Next time you're in my neck of the woods, drop by for a mug of cocoa, you hear?"

With that, Charlie turned and took off.

I turned to Ashley and grinned. "Nice work. You just wrapped up the last loose end!"

Ashley glanced at her watch. "Uh-oh," she said. "We're going to be late for the shoot!"

We hurried on. A few minutes later we arrived at the edge of a small frozen lake. Cameras and lights were set up all around.

Dana called for quiet. The cameraman aimed his camera. Wally lumbered out onto the ice. He reached into a hole in the ice— and pulled out a huge, steaming mug of Polar Cocoa. He slurped it down, grunting happily.

Natasha pointed at Wally. "See? I was right all along!" she exclaimed. "There really was a monster! I told you so!"

I rolled my eyes. Ashley shook her head. Natasha was totally impossible!

But it really didn't matter.

Because the Trenchcoat Twins just cracked another case!

Hi from the both of us,

Ashley and I were on our school basket-ball team, the Mustangs, and we were going for the championship! Nothing could stand in our way...or so we thought.

But then strange things began happening to our team. First our official jerseys were stolen. Then our lockers were glued shut. After that, the team began getting mean notes. And on game night, our star player vanished!

Ashley and I had to get to the bottom of this foul play—before bad luck blew the whistle on our team!

Want to find out more? Check out the next page for a sneak peek at The New Adventures of Mary-Kate & Ashley: *The Case of the Slam Dunk Mystery*.

See you next time!

Love,

Ashley Olsen *& Mary-Kate Olsen*

The Case Of The

SLAM DUNK MYSTERY

The next afternoon, we didn't have basketball practice. That gave us a chance to shadow our number one suspect, Becky. When she walked home from school, we followed her.

We kept near trees and shrubs that lined the sidewalk. We've had a lot of practice following people without getting caught. Detectives have to do it all the time.

At last we reached her house. We hid across the street behind a big blue-and-red mailbox. We watched Becky walk up the steps and go inside.

Ashley looked at me. "Now what?"

"Follow me!" I said. We circled around

to the backyard. I dropped my backpack. "Give me a boost so I can look in the window."

Ashley laced her fingers into a step. I put my foot in and stepped up to look in the window.

"Ouch!" Ashley said. "Mary-Kate—stop wiggling!"

I stretched my neck and peered through the window. I was looking into a sunny, cheerful kitchen.

"There's Becky!" I whispered excitedly.

"What's she doing?" Ashley whispered back.

"Making microwave popcorn!" I whispered.

"That's not a clue," Ashley said. "Ow! You're crushing my fingers, Mary-Kate. I hope she does something suspicious—fast. I can't hold you up much longer!"

Suddenly we heard a man's voice. "I'll be there in a minute, honey."

Uh-oh. Becky's dad! And from the sound of his voice, he was coming around toward the backyard!

"We'd better hide," Ashley whispered. "Or we'll get caught snooping!"

I jumped down. We looked around frantically as we grabbed our packs.

A gravel sidewalk led to a small yellow building at the back of the yard.

"The shed!" I said. We dashed for the little building and quickly ducked inside. It was dark and musty smelling. A small window on one side let in a little sunlight.

We hid behind a lawn mower and several giant bags of potting soil.

"Shhh!" Ashley said.

Footsteps. They were coming this way!

Ashley slipped her hand into mine. I don't know whose was trembling more—mine or hers! What if we got caught hiding in the shed? What if they told our mom and dad?

Then—oh, no! The door creaked open!

Ashley and I held our breath.

Would he see us?

Clang! I nearly jumped a foot when the man tossed a trowel into the shed. But then—

Slam! He closed the door.

I let out a big breath. I turned to Ashley. "We're safe—"

Click!

Uh-oh. "What was that?" I exclaimed.

Ashley's eyes grew wide. "It sounded like a lock clicking shut."

My heart sank all the way down to my toes.

Becky's dad had just locked the shed door. With us inside!

We were trapped!

The Ultimate Fa...

mary-kat

Don't miss

❏ The Case Of The
Great Elephant Escape
❏ The Case Of The
Summer Camp Caper
❏ The Case Of The Surfing Secret
❏ The Case Of The Green Ghost
❏ The Case Of The
Big Scare Mountain Mystery
❏ The Case Of The
Slam Dunk Mystery
❏ The Case Of The
Rock Star's Secret
❏ The Case Of The
Cheerleading Camp Mystery
❏ The Case Of The Flying Phantom
❏ The Case Of The Creepy Castle

❏ The Case Of The Golden Slipper
❏ The Case Of The Flapper 'Napper
❏ The Case Of The High Seas Secret
❏ The Case Of The Logical I Ranch
❏ The Case Of The Dog Camp Mystery
❏ The Case Of The Screaming Scarecro...
❏ The Case Of The Jingle Bell Jinx
❏ The Case Of The Game Show Myster...
❏ The Case Of The Mall Mystery
❏ The Case Of The Weird Science Myst...
❏ The Case Of Camp Crooked Lake

Starring i

❏ Switching Goals
❏ Our Lips Are Sealed
❏ Winning London
❏ School Dance Party
❏ Holiday in the Sun

HarperEntertainment
An Imprint of HarperCollinsPublishers
www.harpercollins.com

 mary-kateandashley.com
America Online Keyword: mary-kateandashley

DUALSTAR
PUBLICATIONS

Books created and produced by Parachute Publishing, L.L.C., in cooperation with Dualstar Publications, a division of Dualstar Entertainment Group, Inc.
TWO OF A KIND © 2002 Warner Bros THE NEW ADVENTURES OF MARY-KATE & ASHLEY and STARRING IN TM & © 2002 Dualstar Entertainment Group, Inc.

eading Checklist

ndashley

gle one!

TWO of a kind

- Twin Thing
- to Flunk
- First Date
- Sleepover Secret
- Twin Too Many
- noop or Not to Snoop?
- ister the Supermodel
- 's a Crowd
- Party!
- ng All Boys
- ner Take All
- Wish You Were Here
- Cool Club
- of the Wardrobes
- Bye Boyfriend
- Snow Problem
- s Me, Likes Me Not
- e Thing
- for the Road

- ❏ Surprise, Surprise
- ❏ Sealed With a Kiss
- ❏ Now You See Him, Now you Don't
- ❏ April Fools' Rules!

so little time

- ❏ How to Train a Boy
- ❏ Instant Boyfriend
- ❏ Too Good To Be True

Mary-Kate and Ashley Sweet 16

- ❏ Never Been Kissed
- ❏ Wishes and Dreams
- ❏ Going My Way

Super Specials:
- ❏ My Mary-Kate & Ashley Diary
- ❏ Our Story
- ❏ Passport to Paris Scrapbook
- ❏ Be My Valentine

**Available wherever books are sold,
or call 1-800-331-3761 to order.**

Mary-Kate and Ashley
Sweet 16

Never Been Kissed

Wishes and Dreams

The Perfect Summer

Getting There

It
Who
YOU
Re

PARACHUTE
PRESS

mary-kateandashley.com
America Online Keyword: mary-kateandashley

DUALSTAR
PUBLICATIONS

Books
for Real
Girls

HarperEntertainment
An Imprint of HarperCollins Pu
www.harpercollins.com

Books created and produced by Parachute Publishing, L.L.C., in cooperation with Dualstar Publications, Inc., a division of Dualstar Entertainment Group, In
America Online and the Triangle logo are registered service marks of America Online, Inc.

ary-Kate and Ashley's
Bestselling Book Series!

so little time
how to train a boy

Mary-Kate Olsen   Ashley Olsen

so little time
instant boyfriend

Win a trip to Hollywood and meet Mary-Kate and Ashley! Details inside.

BASED ON THE HIT TV SERIES

Mary-Kate Olsen   Ashley Olsen

so little time
too good to be true

BASED ON THE HIT TV SERIES

BASED ON THE HIT TV SHOW.

e and Riley... So much to do...   so little time

mary-kateandashley.com
America Online Keyword: mary-kateandashley

DUALSTAR PUBLICATIONS

HarperEntertainment
An Imprint of HarperCollinsPublishers
www.harpercollins.com

Books for Real Girls

ted and produced by Parachute Publishing, L.L.C., in cooperation with Dualstar Publications, Inc., a division of Dualstar Entertainment Group, Inc.
TIME © 2002 Dualstar Entertainment Group, Inc.

MARY-KATE AND ASHLEY *in ACTION!*

26 Action-Packed
Half-Hour Episodes
from Dualstar Animation
and DIC Entertainment
Airing on Disney's
One Saturday Morning on ABC

DUALSTAR
ANIMATION

™ & © 2001 DUALSTAR ENTERTAINMENT GROUP, INC.

Heat up your music collection...

12 great tracks...
including a special version of the hit song
Island in the Sun with background vocals by
Mary-Kate and Ashley.

ALSO FEATURING: ...the hot new single
Us Against The World by Play!

Music From The Motion Picture
mary-kate olsen   ashley olsen
HOLIDAY
IN THE SUN

mary-kateandashley.com
America Online Keyword: mary-kateandashley

DUALSTAR
RECORDS

©2001 Dualstar Entertainment Group, Inc. Distributed by Trauma Records. All rights reserved.

mary-kateandashley.com
America Online Keyword: mary-kateanda

Mary-Kate and Ashley's new movie now available on videocassette and DVD

FILMED AT ATLANTIS
PARADISE ISLAND, BAHAMAS
ATLANTIS.COM

Featuring the hit single
Island in the Sun
And the new *Play* single
Us Against the World

DUALSTAR VIDEO & DVD   TAPESTRY   Distributed

Soundtrack also available on
DUALSTAR RECORDS   TRAUMA RECORDS

mary-kateandashley.com
America Online Keyword: mary-kateandashley

TM & © 2002 Dualstar Entertainment Group, inc. All Rights Reserved.

GAME GIRLS mary-kateandashley
VIDEOGAMES
JOIN IN THE FUN!

Games for Real Girls

PlayStation
CRUSH COURSE
CRUSH COURSE

Available NOW!

GAME BOY COLOR   GAME BOY COLOR   GAME BOY COLOR   PlayStation   PlayStation
get a clue   Packin Planner   WINNERS CIRCLE   GAME

EVERYONE E — ESRB

DUALSTAR INTERACTIVE

mary-kateandashley.com
America Online Keyword: mary-kateandashley

CLUB Acclaim

© & ™ 2002 Dualstar Entertainment Group, Inc. All Rights Reserved. Acclaim © and Club Acclaim™ & © 2002 Acclaim Entertainment, Inc. All Rights Reserved.